Tidying My Room

Written by
Stephen Rickard

I am tidying my room.
Holly is coming to play.

I am picking up my clothes.
My clothes go in the basket.

My toys are on the floor.
I am picking them up
and I am putting them
in the toybox.

My bears are going
in my bed.
"Come on, bears.
You are going to bed."

I am tidying my books.
My books go
on the shelf.
I am picking them up
and I am putting them
on the shelf.

"Look at my tidy room, Holly.
We can play with my toys and my books.
Sh … sh … sh …
My bears are in bed."